Date: 1/19/12

E WAKEMAN
Wakeman, Daniel,
Ben's bunny trouble /

PALM BEACH COUNTY
LIBRARY SYSTEM
3650 Summit Boulevard
West Palm Beach, FL 33406-4198

Ben's Bunny Trouble

For Iva, Jules, Peter, Bugs, Thumper,
Fiver, Bigwig, Uncle Wiggly and Loki.

 Daniel Wakeman  Dirk van Stralen

Orca Book Publishers

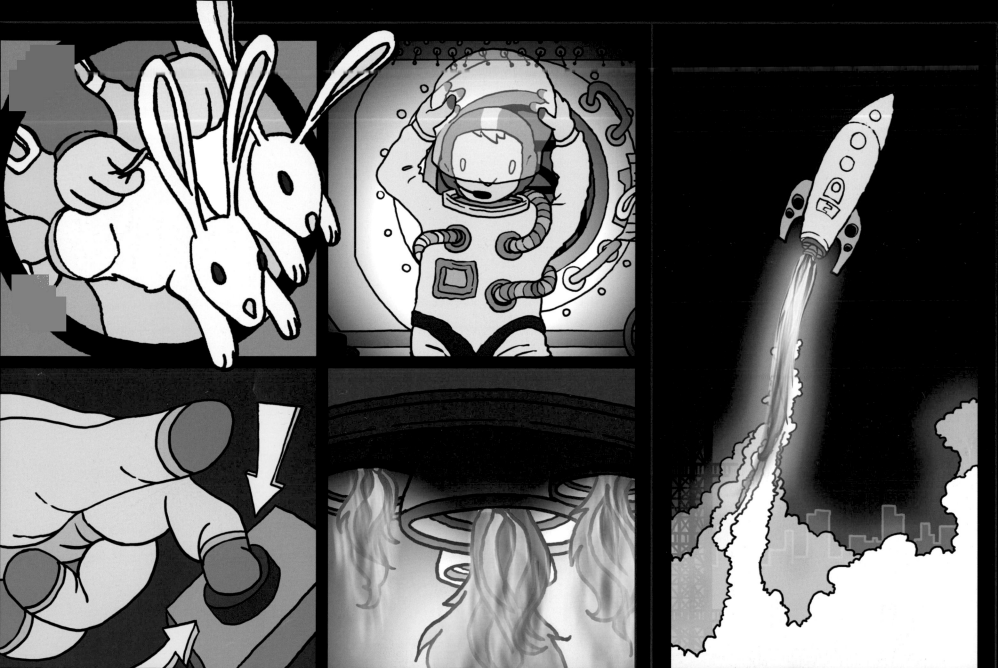

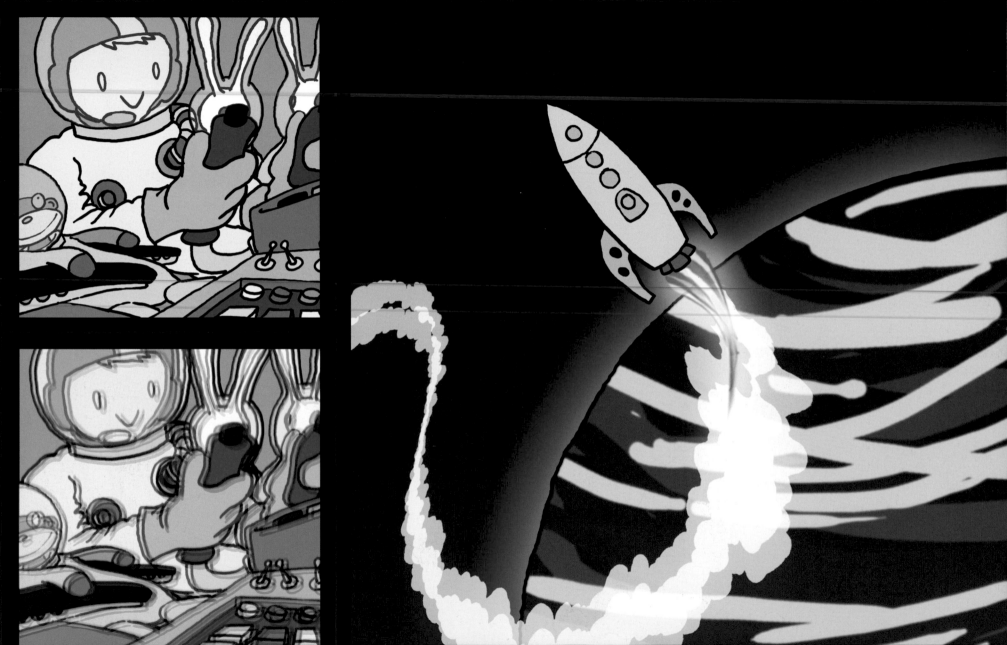

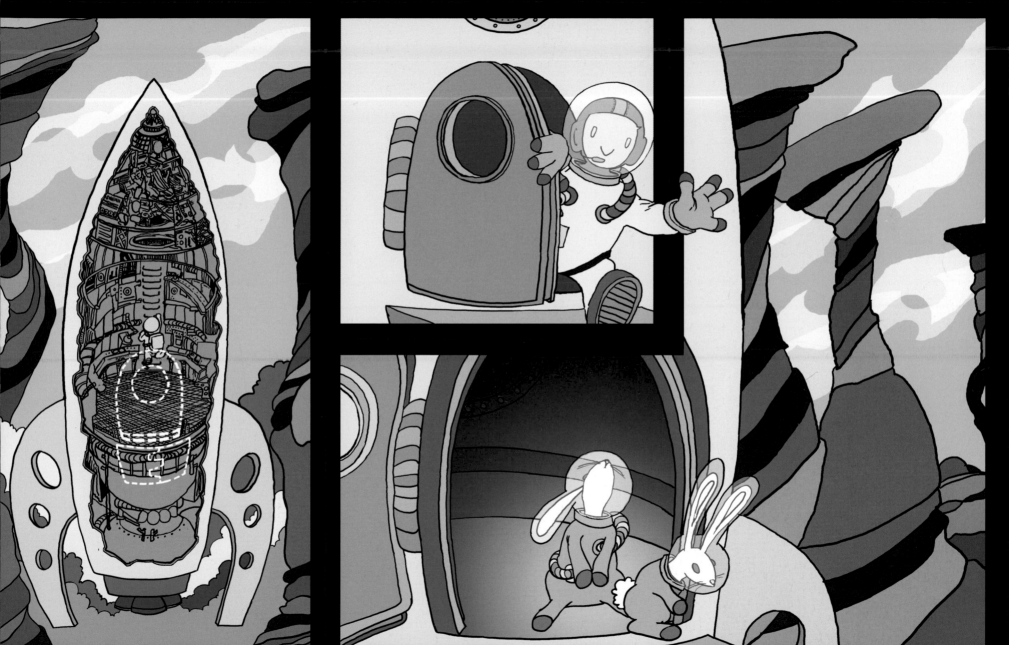

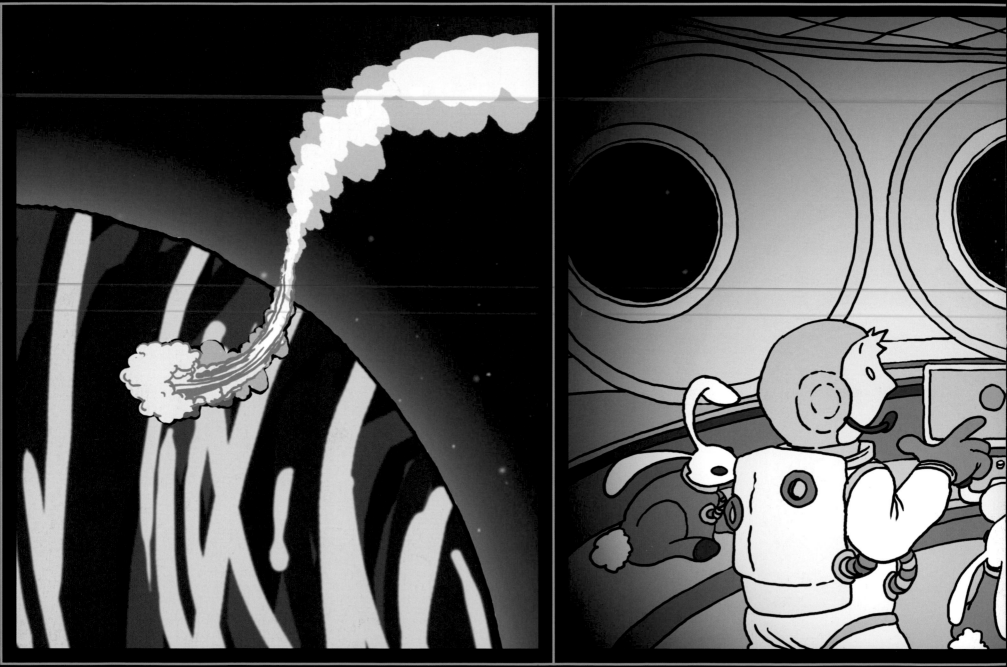

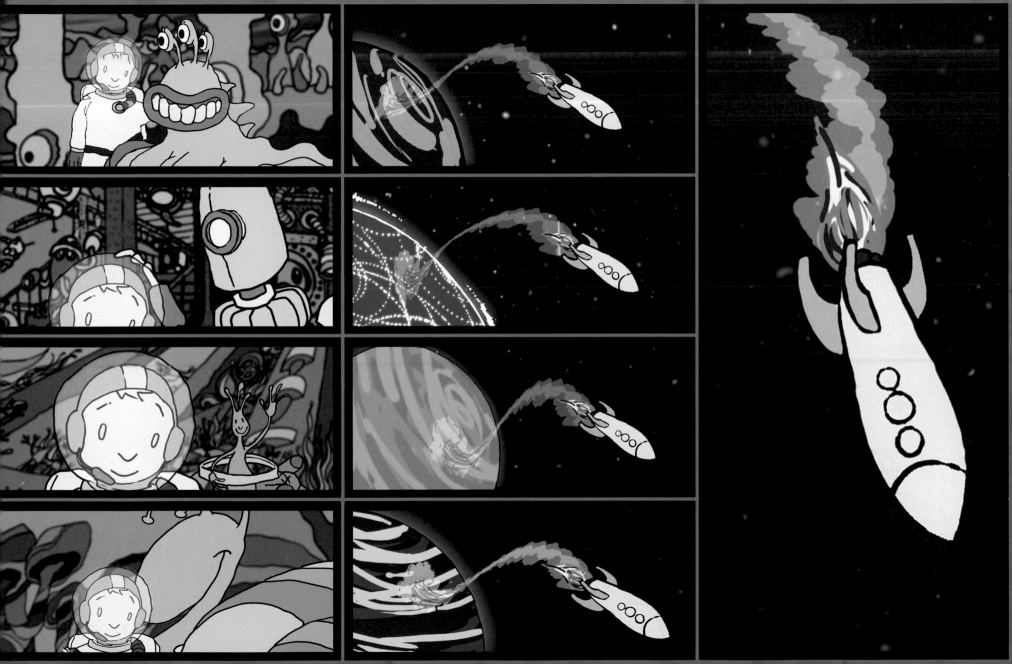

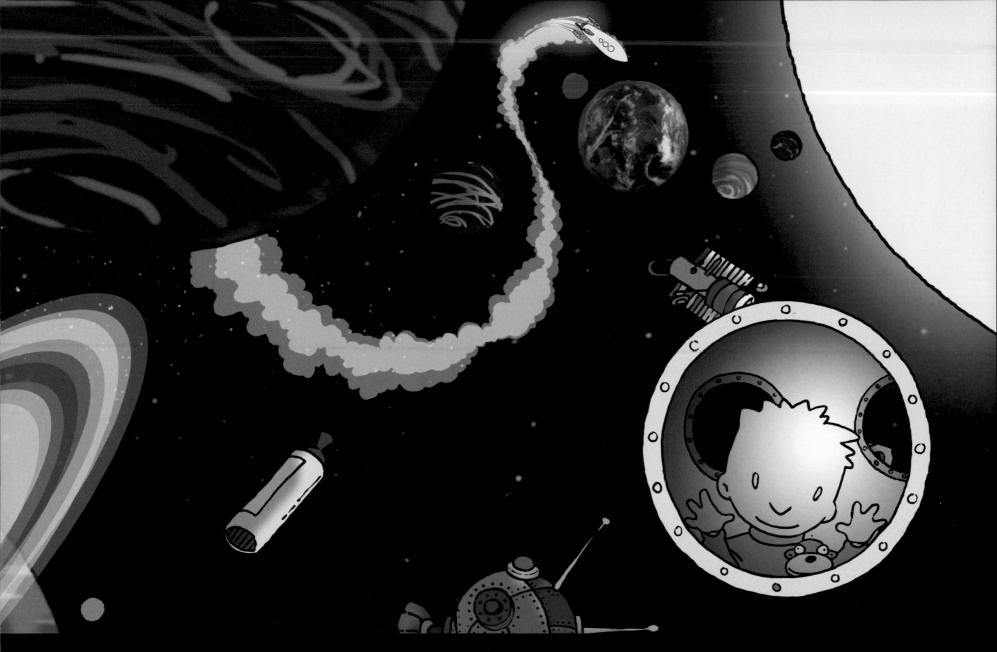

Story copyright © 2007 Daniel Wakeman
Illustrations copyright © 2007 Dirk van Stralen

All rights reserved. No part of this publication may be reproduced or transmitted in
any form or by any means, electronic or mechanical, including photocopying,
recording or by any information storage and retrieval system now known or to be
invented, without permission in writing from the publisher.

Library and Archives Canada Cataloguing in Publication

Wakeman, Daniel, 1967-
Ben's bunny trouble / written by Daniel Wakeman ; illustrated
by Dirk van Stralen.

ISBN 978-1-55143-611-1

1. Rabbits--Juvenile fiction. I. Van Stralen, Dirk, 1966- II. Title.

PS8645.A454B46 2007   jC813'.6   C2007-901850-5

First published in the United States, 2007
Library of Congress Control Number: 2007924934

Summary: In this wordless picturebook, Ben journeys into space to find
his bunnies a better home than his own inhospitable city.

Orca Book Publishers gratefully acknowledges the support for its publishing
programs provided by the following agencies: the Government of Canada through
the Book Publishing Industry Development Program and the Canada Council
for the Arts, and the Province of British Columbia through the BC Arts Council
and the Book Publishing Tax Credit.

Cover design by Dirk van Stralen

Orca Book Publishers   Orca Book Publishers
PO Box 5626, Stn. B   PO Box 468
Victoria, BC Canada   Custer, WA USA
V8R 6S4   98240-0468

www.orcabook.com
Printed and bound in China.
10 09 08 07 • 4 3 2 1